www.mascotbooks.com

For more information, please contact:
Mascot Books
560 Herndon Parkway
Herndon, VA 20170
info@mascotbooks.com

CPSIA Code: PRT0913A
ISBN: 1620864088
ISBN-13: 9781620864081

Library of Congress Control Number: 2013914577

Printed in the United States

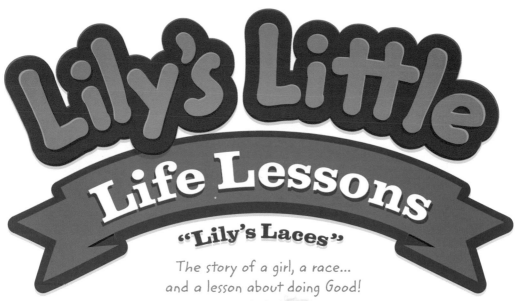

Lily's Little
Life Lessons
"Lily's Laces"

The story of a girl, a race...
and a lesson about doing Good!

Rebecca Perlman
Coniglio, LCSW

Illustrated by
Jen Mundy

Rebecca Perlman Coniglio, LCSW

photo by Jan Press/Photo Media

About the Author:

Rebecca received her Masters in Social Work from the
Columbia University School of Social Work. She is a certified
school social worker and has served on several child study
teams. Rebecca has also worked as an elementary guidance
counselor. Currently, she is in private practice specializing in
children and adolescents. Rebecca lives in New Jersey with
her husband and her very lucky daughter, Lily.

To my Lovely Lily:

In life, keep running races and look for ways to do good along your road.

To Pam and the staff at NJ Sharing Network:

Thank you for taking my call on that May day. I appreciate the time and effort you dedicated to this project. I am honored to give a voice to the cause of raising awareness about organ and tissue donation.

To Veronica:

I have to give credit for the edits. Thank you for dotting my *i*s and crossing my *t*s.

To the children I met at the race:

Thank you for sharing your stories with me and allowing me to bring them to life in this special book. You should feel proud of yourselves. You are an inspiration to all of us.

To Dr. Perez:

Thank you for getting Lily back in running form. We are forever grateful.

To the memory of Maddie:

Your gift was to share. When I see butterflies, I will remember you and smile.

"Daddy, come quick!" I shouted. I looked out my front window, and before my eyes there was a sea of runners.

Daddy flew over to the window and said, "There must be a race today right on our street—this reminds me of when I was on the track team in high school." Mommy smiled at him. I was only four years old then, but I grabbed my sneakers and tugged on the laces—I was ready to run, too.

Mommy said, "You are too little, Lily, but we can go outside and cheer them on." That is exactly what we did. I stood on the curb and waved a green pom-pom a passerby had handed me. It was super fun.

I waited one whole year, and on another warm, June Sunday, the runners came again. This time I was ready on my front steps with my pom-poms.

I loved watching the runners, and I yelled, "Go, go!" and "Good job!" I begged Mommy and Daddy to let me run in the race next year. They said maybe I could do it when I turned six.

Well, guess who is six now? Me — Lucky Lily — and it is my time to run in the race that goes down my street. I'm thrilled, but Mommy says first I have to learn what the race is all about. She loves to teach me life lessons, you know.

Mommy and Daddy explain that an organization called NJ Sharing Network organizes a 5K race for a good cause. I ask, "What is the good cause?" They tell me that sometimes when people go to heaven, they can share certain parts of their bodies called organs.

Did you know that we all have twelve major organs in our bodies, and each organ does an important job to help our bodies work well?

Some organs can be donated to others who are sick and hoping to get better. It is a circle of giving, hope, love, and life.

Here is what I think... we are lucky to be alive, but if we are no longer alive, we can still be lucky because we can be like a superhero and save other people.

From the stars, we can watch over the world,
kind of like the Tooth Fairy.

Mommy tells me the race will be even more special this year because I'm going to get to meet a group of girls who are running to honor the memory of their friend, Maddie. One day before the race I ask Mommy, "Can you tell me more about Maddie?"

"Sure, come on — let's sit down and I will tell you what I know." Maddie was a young girl who was born with a medical condition. She was small in size but had a big spirit. Maddie was brave and kind.

When it was her time to go to heaven, her parents made the loving decision to donate her organs to help others who were in need. They felt it was what Maddie would have wanted. After Maddie was in heaven, her parents found a box in her closet with a note inside that read, "My gift is to share."

"Ooh," I say, "so Maddie is just like one of those superheroes I was talking about. Mommy, can I ask you another question?"

"Of course, Lily. You can ask me anything, always."

"Will there be anyone at the race who is feeling better after receiving a new organ?"

"That's a great question!" A boy named Michael who received a new kidney will be there. Michael is wonderful because he feels lucky to have his new kidney, and he takes really good care of himself. Michael thinks of his kidney as a gift. He eats healthy meals, gets plenty of rest, and takes his medicine. Michael is a fine young man with a bright future.

"I'm so glad that Michael is feeling better and can be at the race, too." As I head upstairs to break in my new pink sneakers, I turn around and see Mommy wipe a tear from her eye. Oh Mommy, my little mommy, she is thinking about Maddie, Michael, and me, too.

"Today is the big day...let's lace up and go!" I exclaim. We get down to where the NJ Sharing Network Foundation's 5k race starts, and I see Nama. She has come out to walk with us, and I am so happy to see her that I give her a big hug.

Here comes Grandma and Grandpa, too; now I'm getting excited. Just then I spot my friends: Patrick, Thomas, Alexander, Giuliana, Christina, and Sofia. Wow, so many people are here to help out the good cause. Is that cotton candy? This is the best day ever!

Mommy says, "Let's go meet Maddie's friends." All of a sudden, I start to feel nervous. What if her friends are sad because they miss Maddie? But then I hear cheering—it is coming from Maddie's friends. They are sad, but happy, too. They are excited to be at the race to share Maddie's story with everyone.

I go over to them and say, "Hi, I am Lily." One of the girls asks me who I am running for today. I'm not sure what to say, but Mommy explains that we are running to honor all the people who are not here anymore and everyone they helped to get well. The girls tell us more about Maddie: she loved cotton candy, too, and swimming.

It's finally time to start the race, but first there is one thing I simply must do. I walk over to Mommy and Daddy and thank them for letting me run today. Mommy hugs me tight, bends down to tighten my laces, and says, "Lily, you inspired me today. I want to stay here with you forever, but if I can't, I will donate my organs to help others be strong long after I'm gone."

Just then, the horn blows—this is it—here we go!

The End.

NJ Sharing Network

saving lives through
organ and tissue donation

Our Mission

NJ Sharing Network is committed to saving and enhancing lives through the miracle of organ and tissue donation and transplantation.

Who We Are

NJ Sharing Network is a non-profit, federally designated organ procurement organization responsible for the recovery of organs and tissue for the 5,000 New Jersey residents currently awaiting transplantation, and is part of the national recovery system, which is in place for the nearly 120,000 people on waiting lists.

Our Foundation

The NJ Sharing Network Foundation is committed to increasing the number of lives saved through education, research, donor family support, and public awareness about the life-saving benefits of organ and tissue donation and transplantation. By making a contribution to the NJ Sharing Network Foundation, you empower our efforts, bringing us a step closer to providing the greatest gift of all: life.

©Photo by Jessica Hatton

5 Ways You Can Help

Register to be a donor

Share this message

Volunteer to help spread the word

Like us on Facebook (NJ Sharing Network) and
Follow us on Twitter (@NJSharing)

Join the Annual 5K Walk and USATF Certified Race!

For more information, please visit us at www.NJSharingNetwork.org

The NJ Sharing Network Foundation is proud to fund the
publication of "Lily's Laces."